THOMAS
and the
Missing Christmas Tree

Christopher Awdry
Illustrated by **Robin Davies**

THOMAS

and the

Missing Christmas Tree

Christopher Awdry
Illustrated by Robin Davies

Every year, a Christmas tree stands on the platform at Tidmouth Station and people sing carols round it. A week before Christmas, Thomas was at the station with Annie and Clarabel.

The Fat Controller was arranging the carol party. "You'll all have jobs to do," he said. "Thomas, I want you to fetch the tree. Gordon will bring the Mayor, and Henry will be in charge of cards, letters and parcels."

Two days before Christmas, the Fat Controller came to see Thomas.
"It's time for you to fetch the tree, Thomas," he said.
"Duck can look after Annie and Clarabel until you get back."
Thomas puffed happily away.

The other engines waited for Thomas to come back.
They waited and waited.
The next morning they were still waiting.

"Perhaps he's stuck in a tunnel somewhere," Gordon suggested.
"Don't mention tunnels!" worried Henry.
"He could have run into a cow . . ." said Donald.

"He has done nothing of the kind," the Fat Controller interrupted. "There has been a heavy snowfall and he seems to be stranded."
"We're not going to leave him, are we?" asked Douglas.
"Certainly not," replied the Fat Controller. "I shall need two volunteers . . ." The noise was deafening!

At once Donald and Douglas
were coupled back to back,
with a van between them and
a snowplough at each end. Cold but
confident, they set out to the rescue.

Donald and Douglas puffed bravely on, but the snow was getting thicker now. They struggled through Edward's station.
Donald wanted to stop for a rest, but Douglas wouldn't let him.
"What if Thomas is lying hurt somewhere?" he said.

Great drifts of snow lay across Gordon's Hill.
Again and again they forced the snowplough into
the snow, each time moving slowly forward.
Then they drew back and paused for breath.
"Shh!" said Douglas suddenly. "I can hear something."

Very faintly came a muffled cry for help.
"It's Thomas!" exclaimed Donald.
"Told you so," said Douglas. "Come on, let's get him out –
he must be frozen solid in there."

Before long, Edward and James arrived with more help.
The men climbed out of their van and set to work.
Thomas was soon clear.

Edward and James pulled Thomas and the precious Christmas tree back to a crossover. Then Donald and Douglas helped him back to Tidmouth along the line they had already cleared. When they all reached Tidmouth, the waiting engines cheered.

The Christmas tree was quickly unloaded, put into its tub and
decorated, just before people began to crowd into the station.
"As a reward for your hard work you may stay and enjoy the
carols," the Fat Controller announced.
James was so pleased that he let off steam suddenly, "Wheesh!"

Next, "One, two, three," boomed the Fat Controller, and suddenly, like magic, the station was flooded with light.
"Three cheers for Thomas the Tank Engine and his Friends!"

As the cheers died away, a whirring noise came from the sky. Everyone looked up – they knew who it was.
With his landing light shining brightly, Harold the Helicopter touched down gently in the snow. Then out stepped a familiar figure wearing a red cloak and hood.
Everyone cheered as Father Christmas gave out the presents to the children and the carol party began.

After a marvellous party, Thomas and his friends went back to the shed together.

"It's no fun getting stuck in the snow," whispered Thomas, "but it was worth it for a party like that. Happy Christmas, everyone!"